W9-BJQ-842

THE BIRTHDAY OF THE INFANTA

F55423

by OSCAR WILDE

with illustrations by LEONARD LUBIN

THE VIKING PRESS New York

Illustrations Copyright © Leonard Lubin, 1979
All rights reserved. First published in 1979 by The Viking Press,
625 Madison Avenue, New York, N.Y. 10022. Published simultaneously in
Canada by Penguin Books Canada Limited. Printed in U.S.A.
1 2 3 4 5 83 82 81 80 79

Library of Congress Cataloging in Publication Data
Wilde, Oscar, 1854-1900. The birthday of the infanta.
Summary: A grotesque dwarf falls in love with the beautiful Infanta.
[1. Fairy tales] I. Lubin, Leonard B. II. Title.
PZ8.W647Bi[Fic]   79-14329   ISBN 0-670-16974-9

For Jane Felton Gray

THE BIRTHDAY
OF THE INFANTA

The tall striped tulips stood straight up upon their stalks.

It was the birthday of the Infanta.

She was just twelve years of age, and the sun was shining brightly in the gardens of the Palace.

Although she was a real Princess and the Infanta of Spain, she had only one birthday every year, just like the children of quite poor people, so it was naturally a matter of great importance to the whole country that she should have a really fine day for the occasion. And a really fine day it certainly was. The tall striped tulips stood straight up upon their stalks, like long rows of soldiers, and looked defiantly across the grass at the roses, and said: "We are quite as splendid as you are now." The purple butterflies fluttered about with gold dust on their wings, visiting each flower in turn; the little lizards crept

3

out of the crevices of the wall and lay basking in the white glare; and the pomegranates split and cracked with the heat and showed their bleeding red hearts. Even the pale yellow lemons, that hung in such profusion from the moldering trellis and along the dim arcades, seemed to have caught a richer color from the wonderful sunlight, and the magnolia trees opened their great globe-like blossoms of folded ivory and filled the air with a sweet, heavy perfume.

The little Princess herself walked up and down the terrace with her companions, and played at hide-and-seek around the stone vases and the old moss-grown statues. On ordinary days she was allowed to play only with children of her own rank, so she had always to play alone, but her birthday was an exception, and the King had given orders that she was to invite any of her young friends whom she liked to come and amuse themselves with her. There was a stately grace about these slim Spanish children as they glided about, the boys with their large-plumed hats and short fluttering cloaks, the

The little Princess herself walked up and down the terrace with her companions.

girls holding up the trains of their long brocade gowns, and shielding the sun from their eyes with huge fans of black and silver. But the Infanta was the most graceful of all, and the most tastefully attired, after the somewhat cumbrous fashion of the day. Her robe was of gray satin, the skirt and the wide puffed sleeves heavily embroidered with silver, and the stiff corset studded with rows of fine pearls. Two tiny slippers with big pink rosettes peeped out beneath her dress as she walked. Pink and pearl was her great gauze fan, and in her hair, which like an aureole of faded gold stood out stiffly around her pale little face, she had a beautiful white rose.

From a window in the Palace the sad, melancholy King watched them. Behind him stood his brother, Don Pedro of Aragon, whom he hated, and his confessor, the Grand Inquisitor of Granada, sat by his side. Sadder even than usual was the King, for as he looked at the Infanta bowing with childish gravity to the assembling courtiers, or laughing behind the fan at the grim Duchess of Albuquerque who always accompanied her, he thought of the

From a window in the Palace the sad, melancholy King watched them.

young Queen, her mother, who but a short time before—so it seemed to him— had come from the gay country of France and had withered away in the somber splendor of the Spanish court, dying just six months after the birth of her child, and before she had seen the almonds blossom twice in the orchard, or plucked the second year's fruit from the old gnarled fig tree that stood in the center of the now grass-grown courtyard. So great had been his love for her that he had not suffered even the grave to hide her from him. She had been embalmed by a Moorish physician, who in return for this service had been granted his life, which for heresy and suspicion of magical practices had been already forfeited, men said, to the Holy Office, and her body was still lying on its tapestried bier in the black marble chapel of the Palace, just as the monks had borne her on that windy March day nearly twelve years before. Once every month the King, wrapped in a dark cloak and with a muffled lantern in his hand, went in and knelt by her side, calling out, *"Mi reina! Mi reina!"* and sometimes breaking through the formal etiquette that in Spain governs every separate action of life and sets limits even to the sorrow of a King, he would clutch at the pale jeweled hands in a wild agony of grief and try to wake by his mad kisses the cold painted face.

Today he seemed to see her again, as he had seen her first at the Castle of Fontainebleau, when he was but fifteen years of age, and she still younger. They had been formally betrothed on that occasion by the Papal Nuncio in the presence of the French King and all the Court, and he had returned to the Escorial bearing with him a little ringlet of yellow hair, and the memory of two childish lips bending down to kiss his hand as he stepped into his carriage. Later on had followed the marriage, hastily performed at Burgos, a small town on the frontier between the two countries, and the grand public entry into Madrid with the customary celebration of High Mass at the Church of La Atocha, and a more than usually solemn auto-da-fé, in which nearly three hundred heretics, among whom were many Englishmen, had been delivered over to the secular arm to be burned.

He would clutch at the pale jeweled hands in a wild agony of grief.

Certainly he had loved her madly, and to the ruin, many thought, of his country, then at war with England for the possession of the empire of the New World. He had hardly ever permitted her to be out of his sight; for her, he had forgotten, or seemed to have forgotten, all grave affairs of State; and, with that terrible blindness that passion brings upon its servants, he had failed to notice that the elaborate ceremonies by which he sought to please her did but aggravate the strange malady from which she suffered. When she died he was, for a time, like one bereft of reason. Indeed, there is no doubt that he would have formally abdicated and retired to the great Trappist monastery at Granada, of which he was already titular Prior, had he not been afraid to leave the little Infanta at the mercy of his brother, whose cruelty, even in Spain, was notorious, and who was suspected by many of having caused the Queen's death by means of a pair of poisoned gloves that he had presented to her on the occasion of her visiting his castle in Aragon. Even after the expiration of the three years of public mourning that he had ordained throughout his whole dominions by royal edict, he would never suffer his ministers to speak about any new alliance, and when the Emperor himself sent to him, and offered him the hand of the lovely Archduchess of Bohemia, his niece, in marriage, he bade the ambassadors tell their master that the King of Spain was already wedded to Sorrow, and that though she was but a barren bride he loved her better than Beauty; an answer that cost his crown the rich provinces of the Netherlands, which soon after, at the Emperor's instigation, revolted against him under the leadership of some fanatics of the Reformed Church.

His whole married life, with its fierce, fiery-colored joys and the terrible agony of its sudden ending, seemed to come back to him today as he watched the Infanta playing on the terrace. She had all the Queen's pretty petulance of manner, the same willful way of tossing her head, the same proud, curved, beautiful mouth, the same wonderful smile—*vrai sourire de France* indeed—as she glanced up now and then at the window, or stretched out her little hand for the stately Spanish gentlemen to kiss. But the shrill laughter of the children grated on his ears, and the bright pitiless sunlight mocked his sorrow, and a dull odor of strange spices, such as embalmers use, seemed to taint—or was it fancy? —the clear morning air. He buried his face in his hands, and when the Infanta looked up again, the curtains had been drawn and the King had retired.

She made a little *moue* of disappointment and shrugged her shoulders. Surely he might have stayed with her on her birthday. What did the stupid State affairs matter? Or had he gone to that gloomy chapel, where the candles were always burning, and where she was never allowed to enter? How silly of him, when the sun was shining so brightly and everybody was so happy! Besides, he would miss the sham bullfight for which the trumpet was already sounding, to say nothing of the puppet show and the other wonderful things. Her uncle and the Grand Inquisitor were much more sensible. They had come out on the terrace and paid her nice compliments. So she tossed her pretty head, and taking Don Pedro by the hand, she walked slowly down the steps toward a long pavilion of purple silk that had been erected at the end of the

Taking Don Pedro by the hand, she walked slowly down the steps.

garden, the other children following in strict order of precedence, those who had the longest names going first.

A procession of noble boys, fantastically dressed as toreadors, came out to meet her, and the young Count of Tierra Nueva, a wonderfully handsome lad of about fourteen years of age, uncovering his head with all the grace of a born hidalgo and grandee of Spain, led her solemnly in to a little gilt and ivory chair that was placed on a raised dais above the arena. The children grouped themselves all around, fluttering their big fans and whispering to each other, and Don Pedro and the Grand Inquisitor stood laughing at the entrance. Even the Duchess—the Camerera Mayor, as she was called—a thin, hard-featured woman with a yellow ruff, did not look quite so bad-tempered as usual, and something like a chill smile flitted across her wrinkled face and twitched her thin, bloodless lips.

It certainly was a marvelous bullfight, and much nicer, the Infanta thought, than the real bullfight that she had been brought to see at Seville, on the occasion of the visit of the Duke of Parma to her father. Some of the boys pranced about on richly caparisoned hobbyhorses, brandishing long javelins with gay streamers of bright ribands attached to them; others went on foot, waving their scarlet cloaks before the bull, and vaulting lightly over the barrier when he charged them; and as for the bull himself, he was just like a live bull, though he was only made of wickerwork and stretched hide, and sometimes insisted on running around the arena on his hind legs, which no live bull ever dreams of doing. He made a splendid fight of it, too, and the children got so excited that they stood up upon the benches and waved their lace handkerchiefs and cried out: *"Bravo toro! Bravo toro!"* just as sensibly as if they had been grown-up people. At last, however, after a prolonged combat, during which several of the hobbyhorses were gored through and through and their riders dismounted, the young Count of Tierra Nueva brought the bull to his knees, and having obtained permission from the Infanta to give the *coup de grâce,* he plunged

Others went on foot, waving their scarlet cloaks before the bull.

his wooden sword into the neck of the animal with such violence that the head came right off and disclosed the laughing face of little Monsieur de Lorraine, the son of the French Ambassador at Madrid.

The arena was then cleared amid much applause, and the dead hobbyhorses dragged solemnly away by two Moorish pages in yellow and black liveries, and after a short interlude, during which a French posture master performed upon a tightrope, some Italian puppets appeared in the semiclassical tragedy of *Sophonisba* on the stage of a small theater that had been built up for the purpose. They acted so well and their gestures were so extremely natural that at the close of the play the eyes of the Infanta were quite dim with tears. Indeed some of the children really cried, and had to be comforted with sweetmeats, and the Grand Inquisitor himself was so affected that he could not help saying to Don Pedro that it seemed to him intolerable that things made simply out of wood and colored wax and worked mechanically by wires should be so unhappy and meet with such terrible misfortunes.

Some Italian puppets appeared on the stage of a small theater.

An African juggler followed, who brought in a large flat basket covered with a red cloth, and having placed it in the center of the arena, he took from his turban a curious reed pipe and blew through it. In a few moments the cloth began to move, and as the pipe grew shriller and shriller two green and gold snakes put out their strange wedge-shaped heads and rose slowly up, swaying to and fro with the music as a plant sways in the water. The children, however, were rather frightened at their spotted hoods and quick darting tongues, and were much more pleased when the juggler made a tiny orange tree grow out of the sand and bear pretty white blossoms and clusters of real fruit; and when he took the fan of the little daughter of the Marquess de Las Torres and changed it into a blue bird that flew all around the pavilion and sang, their delight and amazement knew no bounds. The solemn minuet, too, performed by the dancing boys from the church of Nuestra Señora del Pilar, was charming. The Infanta had never before seen this wonderful ceremony, which takes place every year at Maytime in front of the high altar of the Virgin, and in her honor; and indeed none of the royal family of Spain had entered the great cathedral of Sara-gossa since a mad priest, supposed by many to have been in the pay of Elizabeth of England, had tried to administer a poisoned wafer to the Prince of the Astu-rias. So she had known only by hearsay of "Our Lady's Dance," as it was called, and it certainly was a beautiful sight. The boys wore old-fashioned Court dresses of white velvet, and their curious three-cornered hats were fringed with silver and surmounted with huge plumes of ostrich feathers, the dazzling whiteness of their costumes, as they moved about in the sunlight, being still more accentuated by their swarthy faces and long black hair. Everybody was fascinated by the grave dignity with which they moved through the intricate figures of the dance, and by the elaborate grace of their slow gestures and stately bows, and when they had finished their performance and doffed their great plumed hats to the Infanta, she acknowledged their reverence with much courtesy, and made a vow that she would send a large wax candle to the shrine of Our Lady of Pilar in return for the pleasure that she had given her.

The boys wore old-fashioned Court dresses of white velvet.

A troop of handsome Egyptians—as the gypsies were termed in those days—then advanced into the arena, and sitting down cross-legged in a circle, began to play softly upon their zithers, moving their bodies to the tune, and humming, almost under their breath, a low dreamy air. When they caught sight of Don Pedro, they scowled at him, and some of them looked terrified, for only a few weeks before he had had two of their tribe hanged for sorcery in the market-place at Seville, but the pretty Infanta charmed them as she leaned back, peeping over her fan with her great blue eyes, and they felt sure that one so lovely as she was could never be cruel to anybody. So they played on very gently and just touched the cords of the zithers with their long, pointed nails, and their heads began to nod as though they were falling asleep. Suddenly, with a cry so shrill that all the children were startled, and Don Pedro's hand clutched at the agate pommel of his dagger, they leaped to their feet and whirled madly around the enclosure, beating their tambourines and chanting some wild love song in their strange guttural language. Then, at another signal, they all flung themselves again to the ground and lay there quite still, the dull strumming of the zithers being the only sound that broke the silence. After they had done this several times, they disappeared for a moment and came back, leading a brown shaggy bear by a chain and carrying on their shoulders some little Barbary apes. The bear stood upon his head with the utmost gravity, and the wizened apes played all kinds of amusing tricks with two gypsy boys who seemed to be their masters, and fought with tiny swords, and fired off guns, and went through regular soldiers' drill just like the King's own bodyguard. In fact the gypsies were a great success.

But the funniest part of the whole morning's entertainment was undoubtedly the dancing of the little Dwarf. When he stumbled into the arena, waddling on his crooked legs and wagging his huge misshapen head from side to side, the children went off into a loud shout of delight, and the Infanta herself laughed so much that the Camerera was obliged to remind her that although there were many precedents in Spain for a King's daughter weeping before

They came back, leading a brown shaggy bear by a chain.

her equals, there were none for a Princess of the blood royal making so merry before those who were her inferiors in birth. The Dwarf, however, was really quite irresistible, and even at the Spanish Court, always noted for its cultivated passion for the horrible, so fantastic a little monster had never been seen. It was his first appearance, too. He had been discovered only the day before, running wild through the forest, by two of the nobles who happened to have been hunting in a remote part of the great cork wood that surrounded the town, and had been carried off by them to the Palace as a surprise for the Infanta; his father, who was a poor charcoal burner, being but too well pleased to get rid of so ugly and useless a child. Perhaps the most amusing thing about him was his complete unconsciousness of his own grotesque appearance. Indeed he seemed quite happy and full of the highest spirits. When the children laughed, he laughed as freely and as joyously as any of them, and at the close of each dance he made them each the funniest of bows, smiling and nodding at them just as if he were really one of themselves, and not a little misshapen thing that

———⋅∞⋅———

Nature, in some humorous mood, had fashioned for others to mock at. As for the Infanta, she absolutely fascinated him. He could not keep his eyes off her, and seemed to dance for her alone, and when at the close of the performance, remembering how she had seen the great ladies of the Court throw bouquets to Caffarelli, the famous Italian treble, whom the Pope had sent from his own chapel to Madrid that he might cure the King's melancholy by the sweetness of his voice, she took out of her hair the beautiful white rose and, partly for a jest and partly to tease the Camerera, threw it to him across the arena with her sweetest smile, he took the whole matter quite seriously, and pressing the flower to his rough, coarse lips, he put his hand upon his heart and sank on one knee before her, grinning from ear to ear, and with his little bright eyes sparkling with pleasure.

This so upset the gravity of the Infanta that she kept on laughing long after the little Dwarf had run out of the arena, and she expressed a desire to her uncle that the dance should be immediately repeated. The Camerera,

She took out of her hair the beautiful white rose and threw it to him.

however, on the plea that the sun was too hot, decided that it would be better that Her Highness should return without delay to the Palace, where a wonderful feast had been already prepared for her, including a real birthday cake with her own initials worked all over it in painted sugar and a lovely silver flag waving from the top. The Infanta accordingly rose up with much dignity, and having given orders that the little Dwarf was to dance again for her after the hour of siesta, and conveyed her thanks to the young Count of Tierra Nueva for his charming reception, she went back to her apartments, the children following in the same order in which they had entered.

Now when the little Dwarf heard that he was to dance a second time before the Infanta, and by her own express command, he was so proud that he ran out into the garden, kissing the white rose in an absurd ecstasy of pleasure, and making the most uncouth and clumsy gestures of delight.

The Flowers were quite indignant at his daring to intrude into their beautiful home, and when they saw him capering up and down the walks, and waving his arms above his head in such a ridiculous manner, they could not restrain their feelings any longer.

"He is really far too ugly to be allowed to play in any place where we are," cried the Tulips.

"He should drink poppy juice and go to sleep for a thousand years," said the great scarlet Lilies, and they grew quite hot and angry.

"He is a perfect horror!" screamed the Cactus. "Why, he is twisted and stumpy, and his head is completely out of proportion with his legs. Really he makes me feel prickly all over, and if he comes near me I will sting him with my thorns."

"And he has actually got one of my best blooms," exclaimed the white Rose tree. "I gave it to the Infanta this morning myself, as a birthday present, and he has stolen it from her." And she called out: "Thief, thief, thief!" at the top of her voice.

———◆———

Even the red Geraniums, who did not usually give themselves airs, and were known to have a great many poor relations themselves, curled up in disgust when they saw him, and when the Violets meekly remarked that though he was certainly extremely plain, still he could not help it, they retorted with a good deal of justice that that was his chief defect, and that there was no reason why one should admire a person because he was incurable; and, indeed, some of the Violets themselves felt that the ugliness of the little Dwarf was almost ostentatious, and that he would have shown much better taste if he had looked sad, or at least pensive, instead of jumping about merrily and throwing himself into such grotesque and silly attitudes.

As for the old Sundial, who was an extremely remarkable individual, and had told the time of day to no less a person than the Emperor Charles V himself, he was so taken aback by the little Dwarf's appearance that he almost forgot to mark two whole minutes with his long shadowy finger, and could not help saying to the great milk-white Peacock, who was sunning herself on the balustrade, that everyone knew that the children of Kings were Kings, and that the children of charcoal burners were charcoal burners, and that it was absurd to pretend that it wasn't so; a statement with which the Peacock entirely agreed, and indeed screamed out, "Certainly, certainly," in such a loud harsh voice that the Goldfish who lived in the basin of the cool splashing fountain put their heads out of the water and asked the huge stone Tritons what on earth was the matter.

But somehow the Birds liked him. They had seen him often in the forest, dancing about like an elf after the eddying leaves, or crouched up in the hollow of some old oak tree, sharing his nuts with the squirrels. They did not mind his being ugly a bit. Why, even the Nightingale herself, who sang so sweetly in the orange groves at night that sometimes the Moon leaned down to listen, was not much to look at, after all; and, besides, he had been kind to them, and during that terribly bitter winter, when there were no berries on the trees, and the ground was as hard as iron, and the wolves had come down to the very gates of the city to look for food, he had never once forgotten them, but had always given them crumbs out of his little hunch of black bread, and divided with them whatever poor breakfast he had.

So they flew around and around him, just touching his cheek with their wings as they passed, and chattered to each other, and the little Dwarf was so pleased that he could not help showing them the beautiful white rose, and telling them that the Infanta herself had given it to him because she loved him.

They did not understand a single word of what he was saying, but that made no matter, for they put their heads on one side, and looked wise, which is quite as good as understanding a thing, and very much easier.

The Lizards also took an immense fancy to him, and when he grew tired of running about and flung himself down on the grass to rest, they played and romped all over him, and tried to amuse him in the best way they could. "Everyone cannot be as beautiful as a lizard," they cried; "that would be too much to expect. And, though it sounds absurd to say so, he is really not

The little Dwarf was so pleased that he could not help
showing them the beautiful white rose.

so ugly after all, provided, of course, that one shuts one's eyes and does not look at him." The Lizards were extremely philosophical by nature, and often sat thinking for hours and hours together, when there was nothing else to do, or when the weather was too rainy for them to go out.

The Flowers, however, were excessively annoyed at their behavior, and at the behavior of the Birds. "It only shows," they said, "what a vulgarizing effect this incessant rushing and flying about has. Well-bred people always stay in exactly the same place, as we do. No one ever saw us hopping up and down the walks, or galloping madly through the grass after dragonflies. When we want a change of air, we send for the gardener, and he carries us to another bed. This is dignified, and as it should be. But birds and lizards have no sense of repose, and indeed birds have not even a permanent address. They are mere vagrants like the gypsies, and should be treated in exactly the same manner." So they put their noses in the air, and looked very haughty, and were quite delighted when after some time they saw the little Dwarf scramble up from the grass and make his way across the terrace to the Palace.

"He should certainly be kept indoors for the rest of his natural life," they said. "Look at his hunched back and his crooked legs," and they began to titter.

But the little Dwarf knew nothing of all this. He liked the birds and the lizards immensely, and thought that the flowers were the most marvelous things in the whole world, except of course the Infanta, but then she had given him the beautiful white rose, and she loved him, and that made a great difference. How he wished that he had gone back with her! She would have put him on her right hand and smiled at him, and he would have never left her side, but would have made her his playmate and taught her all kinds of delightful tricks. For though he had never been in a palace before, he knew a great many wonderful things. He could make little cages out of rushes for the grasshoppers to sing in, and fashion the long-jointed bamboo into the pipe that Pan loves to hear. He knew the cry of every bird, and could call the starlings from the treetop, or the heron from the mere. He knew the trail of every animal, and could track the hare by its delicate footprints, and the boar by the trampled leaves. All the wild dances he knew: the mad dance in red raiment with the autumn, the light dance in blue sandals over the corn, the dance with white snow wreaths in winter, and the blossom dance, through the orchards in spring. He knew where the wood pigeons built their nests, and once when a fowler had snared the parent birds, he had brought up the young ones himself, and had built a little dovecot for them in the cleft of a pollard elm. They were quite tame and used to feed out of his hands every morning. She would like them, and the rabbits that scurried about in the long fern, and the jays with their steely feathers and black bills, and the hedgehogs that could curl themselves up into prickly balls, and the great wise tortoises that crawled slowly about, shaking their heads and nibbling at the young leaves. Yes, she must certainly come to the forest and play with him. He would give her his own little bed, and would watch outside the window till dawn, to see that the wild, horned cattle did not harm her, or the gaunt wolves creep too near the hut. And at dawn he would tap at the shutters and wake her, and they would go out and dance together all the day long. It was really not a bit lonely in the forest. Sometimes a Bishop rode through on his white mule, reading out of a painted book. Sometimes, in their green velvet caps and their jerkins of tanned deerskin, the falconers passed by, with hooded hawks on their wrists. At vintagetime came the grape treaders, with purple hands and feet, wreathed with glossy ivy and carrying dripping skins of wine; and the charcoal burners sat around their huge braziers at night, watching the dry logs charring slowly in the fire, and roasting chestnuts in the ashes, and the robbers came out of their caves and made merry with them. Once, too, he had seen a beautiful procession winding up the long dusty road to Toledo. The monks went in front, singing sweetly and carrying bright banners and crosses of gold, and then, in silver armor, with matchlocks and pikes, came the soldiers, and in their midst walked three barefoot men, in strange yellow dresses painted all over with wonderful figures, and carrying lighted candles in their hands. Certainly there was a great deal to look at in the forest, and when she was tired he would find a soft bank of moss for her, or carry her in his arms, for he was very strong, though he knew that he was not tall. He would make her a necklace of red bryony berries that would be quite as pretty as the white berries that she wore on her dress, and when she was tired of them, she could throw them away, and he would find her others. He would bring her acorn cups and dew-drenched anemones, and tiny glowworms to be stars in the pale gold of her hair.

But where was she? He asked the white rose, and it made him no answer. The whole Palace seemed asleep, and even where the shutters had not been closed, heavy curtains had been drawn across the windows to keep out the glare. He wandered all around, looking for some place through which he might gain an entrance, and at last he caught sight of a little private door that was lying open. He slipped through and found himself in a splendid hall, far more splendid, he feared, than the forest, there was so much more gilding

He slipped through and found himself in a splendid hall.

everywhere, and even the floor was made of great colored stones, fitted together into a sort of geometrical pattern. But the little Infanta was not there, only some wonderful white statues that looked down on him from their jasper pedestals, with sad blank eyes and strangely smiling lips.

At the end of the hall hung a richly embroidered curtain of black velvet, powdered with suns and stars, the King's favorite devices, and embroidered on the color he loved best. Perhaps she was hiding behind that? He would try at any rate.

So he stole quietly across and drew it aside. No, there was only another room, though a prettier room, he thought, than the one he had just left. The walls were hung with a many-figured green arras of needlewrought tapestry representing a hunt, the work of some Flemish artists who had spent more than seven years in its composition. It had once been the chamber of Jean le Fou, as he was called, that mad King who was so enamored of the chase that he had often tried in his delirium to mount the huge rearing horses, and to drag down the stag on which the great hounds were leaping, sounding his hunting horn, and stabbing with his dagger at the pale flying deer. It was now used as the council room, and on the center table were lying the red portfolios of the ministers, stamped with the gold tulips of Spain, and with the arms and emblems of the House of Hapsburg.

The little Dwarf looked in wonder all around him, and was half afraid to go on. The strange silent horsemen that galloped so swiftly through the long glades without making any noise seemed to him like those terrible phantoms of whom he had heard the charcoal burners speaking—the Comprachos, who hunt only at night, and if they meet a man, turn him into a hind and chase him. But he thought of the pretty Infanta and took courage. He wanted to find her alone and to tell her that he too loved her. Perhaps she was in the room beyond.

He ran across the soft Moorish carpets and opened the door. No! She was not here either. The room was quite empty.

The walls were hung with a many-figured green arras of needlewrought tapestry.

———————

It was a throne room, used for the reception of foreign ambassadors, when the King, which of late had not been often, consented to give them a personal audience; the same room in which, many years before, envoys had appeared from England to make arrangements for the marriage of their Queen, then one of the Catholic sovereigns of Europe, with the Emperor's eldest son. The hangings were of gilt Cordovan leather, and a heavy gilt chandelier with branches for three hundred wax lights hung down from the black and white ceiling. Underneath a great canopy of gold cloth, on which the lions and towers of Castile were embroidered in seed pearls, stood the throne itself, covered with a rich pall of black velvet studded with silver tulips and elaborately fringed with silver and pearls. On the second step of the throne was placed the kneeling stool of the Infanta, with its cushion of cloth-of-silver tissue, and below that again, and beyond the limit of the canopy, stood the chair for the Papal Nuncio, who alone had the right to be seated in the King's presence on the occasion of any public ceremonial, and whose Cardinal's hat, with its tangled scarlet tassels,

The throne itself, covered with a rich pall of black velvet studded with silver tulips and elaborately fringed with silver and pearls.

lay on a purple taboret in front. On the wall facing the throne hung a life-sized portrait of Charles V in hunting dress, with a great mastiff by his side, and a picture of Philip II receiving the homage of the Netherlands occupied the center of the other wall. Between the windows stood a black ebony cabinet, inlaid with plates of ivory, on which the figures from Holbein's *Dance of Death* had been graved—by the hand, some said, of that famous master himself.

But the little Dwarf cared nothing for all this magnificence. He would not have given his rose for all the pearls on the canopy, or one white petal of his rose for the throne itself. What he wanted was to see the Infanta before she went down to the pavilion, and to ask her to come away with him when he had finished his dance. Here, in the Palace, the air was close and heavy, but in the forest the wind blew free, and the sunlight with wandering hands of gold moved the tremulous leaves aside. There were flowers, too, in the forest, not so splendid, perhaps, as the flowers in the garden, but more sweetly scented for all that; hyacinths in early spring that flooded with waving purple the cool glens and grassy knolls; yellow primroses that nestled in little clumps around the gnarled roots of the oak trees; bright celandine, and blue speedwell, and irises lilac and gold. There were gray catkins on the hazels, and the foxgloves drooped with the weight of their dappled bee-haunted cells. The chestnut had its spires of white stars, and the hawthorn its pallid moons of beauty. Yes: surely she would come if he could only find her! She would come with him to the fair forest, and all day long he would dance for her delight. A smile lighted up his eyes at the thought, and he passed into the next room.

Of all the rooms this was the brightest and the most beautiful. The walls were covered with a pink-flowered Lucca damask, patterned with birds and dotted with dainty blossoms of silver; the furniture was of massive silver, festooned with florid wreaths and swinging cupids; in front of the two large fireplaces stood great screens embroidered with parrots and peacocks, and the floor, which was of sea-green onyx, seemed to stretch far away into the distance. Nor was he alone. Standing under the shadow of the doorway, at the extreme end of the room, he saw a little figure watching him. His heart trembled, a cry of joy broke from his lips, and he moved out into the sunlight. As he did so, the figure moved out also, and he saw it plainly.

The Infanta! It was a monster, the most grotesque monster he had ever beheld. Not properly shaped as all other people were, but hunchbacked, and crooked-limbed, with huge lolling head and mane of black hair. The little Dwarf frowned, and the monster frowned also. He laughed, and it laughed with him and held its hands to its sides, just as he himself was doing. He made it a mocking bow, and it returned him a low reverence. He went toward it, and it came to meet him, copying each step that he made, and stopping when he stopped himself. He shouted with amusement and ran forward and reached out his hand, and the hand of the monster touched his, and it was as cold as ice. He grew afraid and moved his hand across, and the monster's hand followed it quickly. He tried to press on, but something smooth and hard stopped him. The face of the monster was now close to his own and seemed full of terror. He brushed his hair off his eyes. It imitated him. He struck at it, and it returned blow for blow. He loathed it, and it made hideous faces at him. He drew back, and it retreated.

What was it? He thought for a moment and looked around at the rest of the room. It was strange, but everything seemed to have its double in this invisible wall of clear water. Yes, picture for picture was repeated, and couch for couch. The sleeping Faun that lay in the alcove by the doorway had its twin brother that slumbered, and the silver Venus that stood in the sunlight held out her arms to a Venus as lovely as herself.

Was it Echo? He had called to her once in the valley, and she had answered him word for word. Could she mock the eye, as she mocked the voice? Could she make a mimic world just like the real world? Could the shadows of things have color and life and movement? Could it be that—

He started, and taking from his breast the beautiful white rose, he turned around and kissed it. The monster had a rose of its own, petal for petal the same! It kissed it with like kisses, and pressed it to its heart with horrible gestures.

When the truth dawned upon him, he gave a wild cry of despair and fell sobbing to the floor. So it was he who was misshapen and hunchbacked, foul to look at and grotesque. He himself was the monster, and it was at him that all the children had been laughing, and the little Princess who he had thought loved him—she, too, had been merely mocking at his ugliness and making merry over his twisted limbs. Why had they not left him in the forest, where there was no mirror to tell him how loathsome he was? Why had his father not killed him, rather than sell him to his shame? The hot tears poured down his cheeks, and he tore the white rose to pieces. The sprawling monster did the same, and scattered the faint petals in the air. It groveled on the floor, and, when he looked at it, it watched him with a face drawn with pain. He crept away, lest he should see it, and covered his eyes with his hands. He crawled,

The monster had a rose of its own, petal for petal the same!

like some wounded thing, into the shadow, and lay there moaning.

And at that moment the Infanta herself came in with her companions through the open window, and when they saw the ugly little Dwarf lying on the floor and beating it with his clenched hands, in the most fantastic and exaggerated manner, they went off into shouts of happy laughter, and stood all around him and watched him.

"His dancing was funny," said the Infanta, "but his acting is funnier still. Indeed, he is almost as good as the puppets, only, of course, not quite so natural." And she fluttered her big fan and applauded.

But the little Dwarf never looked up, and his sobs grew fainter and fainter, and suddenly he gave a curious gasp and clutched his side. And then he fell back again and lay quite still.

"That is capital," said the Infanta, after a pause, "but now you must dance for me."

"Yes," cried all the children, "you must get up and dance, for you are as clever as the Barbary apes, and much more ridiculous."

But the little Dwarf made no answer.

And the Infanta stamped her foot, and called out to her uncle, who was walking on the terrace with the Chamberlain, reading some dispatches that had just arrived from Mexico, where the Holy Office had recently been established. "My funny little Dwarf is sulking," she cried. "You must wake him up and tell him to dance for me."

They smiled at each other and sauntered in, and Don Pedro stooped down and slapped the Dwarf on the cheek with his embroidered glove. "You must dance," he said, "*petit monstre*. You must dance. The Infanta of Spain and the Indies wishes to be amused."

But the little Dwarf never moved.

"A whipping master should be sent for," said Don Pedro wearily, and he went back to the terrace. But the Chamberlain looked grave, and he knelt beside the little Dwarf and put his hand upon his heart. And after a few

"For the future, let those who come to play with me have no hearts."

moments he shrugged his shoulders and rose up, and having made a low bow to the Infanta, he said:

"*Mi bella Princesa,* your funny little Dwarf will never dance again. It is a pity, for he is so ugly that he might have made the King smile."

"But why will he not dance again?" asked the Infanta, laughing.

"Because his heart is broken," answered the Chamberlain.

And the Infanta frowned, and her dainty rose-leaf lips curled in pretty disdain. "For the future, let those who come to play with me have no hearts," she cried, and she ran out into the garden.

About This Book

———◦⨯◦———

LEONARD LUBIN prepared the artwork for *The Birthday of the Infanta* using a rapidograph pen and India ink on Bristol plate finish paper. The art was then photographed and printed with an especially strong black ink. The text type is 12 point Linotype Granjon, and the display type is Foundry Deepdene.

F55423

7.95

j FICTION

Wilde, Oscar.
    The birthday of the infanta.

I. Title.

JUN 30 1980 S

1982 1982

BB
CC

Please Do Not Remove Card From Pocket

YOUR LIBRARY CARD
may be used at all library agencies. You
are, of course, responsible for all materials
checked out on it. As a courtesy to others
please return materials promptly — before
overdue penalties are imposed.

The SAINT PAUL PUBLIC LIBRARY

DEMCO